P9-CML-482

How Robin
Saved Spring

Debbie Ouellet

illustrated by Nicoletta Ceccoli

Christy Ottaviano Books

HENRY HOLT AND COMPANY · NEW YORK

Long ago, in a little cottage, there lived two sisters, Lady Winter and Sister Spring. The day came, as it had every year since the beginning of time, for Lady Winter to step aside. Soon Sister Spring would wake from her nine-month sleep to cover the world in every shade of green.

The thought of a dreamless sleep through the lonely months ahead made Lady Winter frown. She lifted her face to the falling snow. Flakes fell like tears from her cheeks.

"The cold white of snow and blue of ice are the only colors for me," Lady Winter said with a sigh. "That pretty little sister of mine thinks her spring is so much better. Who needs pink and yellow flowers? What good are hummingbirds flitting through the trees? A perfect world would be cold and white every day of the year."

Lady Winter slid a slender finger along her regal nose.
She tugged at her long silvery braid. "If I think hard enough,
perhaps I can find a way to make it winter forever."

Lady Winter tiptoed into the room where Sister Spring
lay sleeping in her bed. Her wild tangle of curls spilled
across a leafy pillow.

"How pretty she looks in sleep," said Lady Winter.
"It would be a shame to wake her." Then she smiled a slow,
thoughtful smile.

Out of her magic basket, she pulled a shining ball of yarn.
All through the evening, her chair rocked and creaked.
Click. Click. Click. Her knitting needles moved back and
forth. By morning, Lady Winter had knit a cold white
blanket and several smaller ones.

She crept into Sister Spring's room and gently placed the
blanket over her sister. "So long as you wear this, you will
sleep." Lady Winter brushed a stray lock of hair from Sister
Spring's forehead. "Sleep well, little sister."

$\mathcal{R}$obin sat on the windowsill of the little cottage. With his plain brown belly pressed against the windowpane, he watched everything that Lady Winter did. "Oh no!" he cried. "Sister Spring mustn't sleep forever! What will we do without spring?" He spread his wings and soared up into the sky. "I must get help."

He called all the forest creatures together. He called Bear and Beaver, Skunk and Squirrel. He called Caterpillar, Ladybug, and Snake. He called Maple Tree, River, and Wind. "Listen to me!" Robin shouted. "We must find a way to wake Sister Spring."

Bear's black nose snuffled through a bush for some berries. "I'm big and powerful," he boasted. "I will wake her."

Robin discussed Bear's plan with the other forest creatures. They agreed Bear should be the first to try.

*B*ear waited until nighttime. He crept into the cottage.
Bump! Clatter! Thump! Bear was big and clumsy. Lady
Winter heard him lumbering about. She grabbed the handle
of a broom and chased him out the door.

"You need to be taught a lesson," she scolded. Lady
Winter waved her slim arms over her head. She chanted a
raspy song that stole all the berries from the bushes.

Then she put a white sleeping blanket over Bear. He crawled inside a cave and fell into a deep sleep.

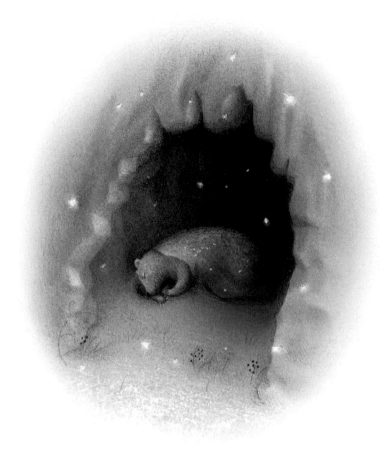

*T*he forest creatures heard of Bear's failure.

"Who will try next?" Robin asked.

"I will," said Caterpillar. "Bear was too big. I am small and can sneak around better."

Squish-a-squish. Caterpillar inched through a crack in the door. But he was bold. He slinked into the house in bright daylight. Lady Winter was waiting. She wagged a finger in front of her nose. "No one fools me."

This time she sang a song that stole all the remaining leaves from the trees so Caterpillar would have nothing to eat. Then she wrapped him in some yarn and hung him from Maple Tree.

*M*aple Tree sent word to Robin. "Let me try next," he said.

Maple Tree asked Wind to help him. *Whirl! Whoosh!* Wind began to blow.

Slap! Tap! Rap! Maple Tree banged on the cottage window as hard as he could. "Surely, this will wake Sister Spring," he said.

Lady Winter shook her head slowly. "You will cry for this," she promised. "Sweet tears for others to drink." She sang another song, this time high-pitched and syrupy.

Soon Maple Tree felt the sugary tears start to fall. They flowed and oozed out of his trunk.

"Who will try now?" Robin asked the forest creatures.

Ladybug poked her head out from under a twig. "Perhaps I could," she said. "My tiny red body can hide in the floor cracks."

Ladybug shuffled into the cottage. *Wriggle. Squeeze. Squiggle.* She inched through the room until she reached the fireplace.

"Who's there?" Lady Winter's voice made her stop.

"Oh dear," Ladybug whispered. "I can't let her see me." She found a pile of cinders near the fire and buried herself. Soon the warm cinders became hot. Ladybug scurried out of the pile. The cinders burned little black spots on her back.

"Sneaking about, little one?" asked Lady Winter. Her giant hand reached down.

Ladybug squeezed through a hole in the wall. She burrowed into the dust balls until she was out of reach.

"If you like my wall so much," said Lady Winter, "you can stay there." Then she sealed the hole so that Ladybug couldn't get out.

Skunk volunteered next. "I'll steal in at night," he told Robin. "My beautiful black coat will blend into the shadows."

Just as the moon slipped behind a cloud, Skunk began to dig. *Scratch. Burrow. Scratch.* He dug a large hole and squeezed under the cottage door.

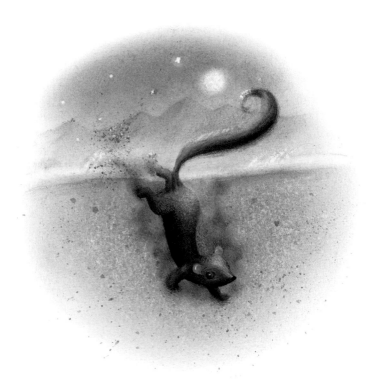

Skunk moved silently, keeping to the dark corners. Just as he reached Sister Spring's bed, he heard a low voice.

"Will you creatures never learn?" Lady Winter ran her hand across his back. A band of snow-white frost stuck where it touched Skunk's fur.

"You foolish little fellow. You won't be sneaking in the dark again." One crystal tear fell from her cheek and shattered on the floor.

Lady Winter put a sleeping blanket over Skunk, too.

"Oh dear!" cried Robin. "Will it be winter forever?"

Then Robin thought of a plan. "Lady Winter is smart," he said. I shall have to trick her. He flew until he found Lady Winter sprinkling frost from her pouch onto the bare trees.

"I've had enough of this!" he shouted so she could hear him. "It's too cold and too white. I am flying away and never coming back!" Then he soared straight up into the sky.

Up, up, up, Robin went. Soon the clouds were far below. He soared past the moon and stars. He didn't stop until he found Mother Sun.

"Mother Sun," he called, "will you give me some morning light to wake Sister Spring?"

Mother Sun creased her forehead and considered his request. "That depends," she said. "Morning light is precious. What will you give me in return?"

Robin thought hard. The only thing he owned of value was his beautiful singing voice. "I shall give you my voice," he said. *Chir-up, chir-ee, tweedle-ee-dee.* He sang the grandest song ever heard.

When the song was finished, Mother Sun's smile glowed bright yellow. "Very well," she said, "but you must come and take the morning light yourself."

Robin flew closer. The heat made it hard to breathe.
He winced as the feathers on his belly caught fire. His
plain brown belly turned a bright orange-red.

    As quickly as he could, Robin grabbed the morning
light and headed back to the forest.

Robin crept to the window of the little cottage. *Tap! Tap! Tap!* He rapped with his beak on the windowpane. He shone the morning light into Sister Spring's eyes and called, "UP! UP! UP!"

Sister Spring stretched and yawned. She opened her violet eyes and smiled at Robin. "Thank you, Robin," she said. "That was a fine sleep, but now I must get to work and make things grow."

Then Sister Spring woke Bear and Skunk from their long winter sleep. She returned the leaves to the trees and berries to the bushes. She released Ladybug from the cottage wall. Sister Spring found Caterpillar and unwrapped the yarn. She gave him beautiful colored wings to thank him for his bravery. She dried Maple Tree's tears.

Spring came back to the world. Grass covered the ground with green. Flowers poked their pink and yellow heads through the earth. Hummingbirds flitted about the trees once more.

Lady Winter stood at the cottage door and scowled at Robin. "Never let me catch you." Then she slowly closed the door behind her.

"Oh dear," said Robin, "from now on, I'll need to be careful." He flew into the forest, vowing to stay out of winter's way.

That is why to this day you will never find a robin in the winter. His belly is red. And if you listen carefully, every spring you will hear him call, "UP! UP! UP!"

To Alex and Sarah with love —D. O.

A mia nonna Italia —N. C.

Henry Holt and Company, LLC, *Publishers since 1866*
175 Fifth Avenue, New York, New York 10010
www.HenryHoltKids.com

Henry Holt® is a registered trademark of Henry Holt and Company, LLC.
Text copyright © 2009 by Debbie Ouellet
Illustrations copyright © 2009 by Nicoletta Ceccoli
All rights reserved.
Distributed in Canada by H. B. Fenn and Company Ltd.

Library of Congress Cataloging-in-Publication Data
Ouellet, Debbie.
How Robin saved spring / Debbie Ouellet ; illustrated by Nicoletta Ceccoli.—1st ed.
p.   cm.
Summary: When Lady Winter casts a sleeping spell on Sister Spring, Robin and the other forest animals
try one by one to sneak past Lady Winter and awaken her sister, so that spring will finally arrive.
ISBN-13: 978-0-8050-6970-9 / ISBN-10: 0-8050-6970-4
[1. Fairy tales. 2. Winter—Fiction. 3. Spring—Fiction.
4. Forest animals—Fiction.] I. Ceccoli, Nicoletta, ill. II. Title.
PZ8.O92Ho 2009   [E]—dc22   2008013424

First Edition—2009 / Designed by Véronique Lefèvre Sweet
Printed in China on acid-free paper. ∞
The artist used acrylics on Fabriano paper to create the illustrations for this book.

1 3 5 7 9 10 8 6 4 2